Sad Days, Glad Days

A Story about Depression

by DeWitt Hamilton
illustrated by Gail Owens

Albert Whitman & Company
Morton Grove, Illinois

This book is for Dick, Jennifer, and Allison. It is also dedicated to parents who have experienced the helpless pain of responding to a child with a frowning face and lethargic limbs instead of the joy we so wish we could give—and continue to strive toward. D.H.

I am very grateful to Bill Hayes and David Ingalls for sharing their professional insights with me; also, special thanks to Penny and Debbie and to the group in Vero, whose help was indispensable. And, always, thanks to Tom Geoly. G.O.

Library of Congress Cataloging-in-Publication Data
Hamilton, DeWitt.
Sad days, glad days : a story about depression /
DeWitt Hamilton ; illustrated by Gail Owens.
p.   cm.
Summary: Amanda Martha tries to understand
her mother's depression, which sometimes
makes her mother sleep all day, feel sad, or cry.
ISBN 0-8075-7200-4
[1. Depression, Mental—Fiction. 2. Mothers and
daughters—Fiction.]   I. Owens, Gail, ill.
II. Title.
PZ7.H181345Sad 1995
[E]—dc20
94-25540
CIP
AC

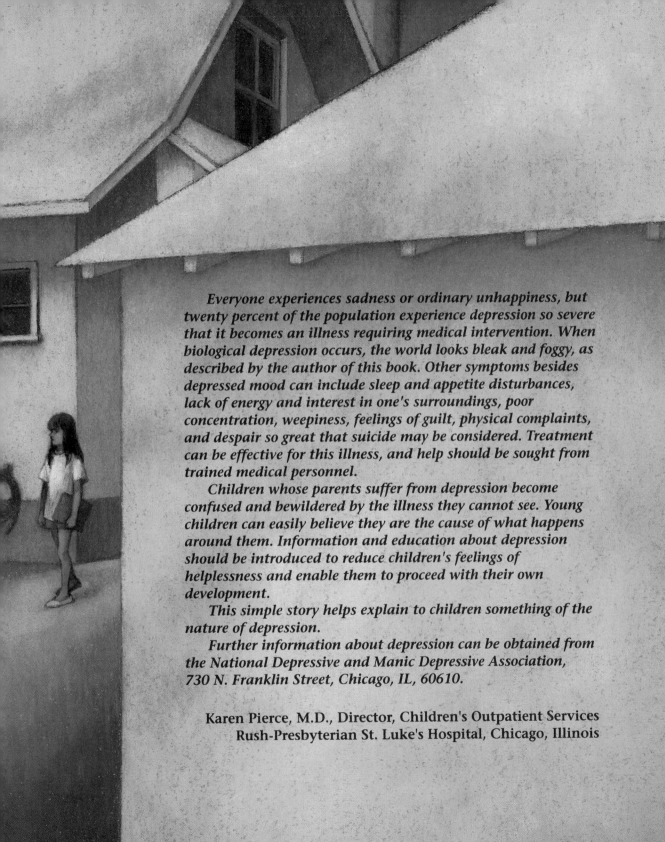

Everyone experiences sadness or ordinary unhappiness, but twenty percent of the population experience depression so severe that it becomes an illness requiring medical intervention. When biological depression occurs, the world looks bleak and foggy, as described by the author of this book. Other symptoms besides depressed mood can include sleep and appetite disturbances, lack of energy and interest in one's surroundings, poor concentration, weepiness, feelings of guilt, physical complaints, and despair so great that suicide may be considered. Treatment can be effective for this illness, and help should be sought from trained medical personnel.

Children whose parents suffer from depression become confused and bewildered by the illness they cannot see. Young children can easily believe they are the cause of what happens around them. Information and education about depression should be introduced to reduce children's feelings of helplessness and enable them to proceed with their own development.

This simple story helps explain to children something of the nature of depression.

Further information about depression can be obtained from the National Depressive and Manic Depressive Association, 730 N. Franklin Street, Chicago, IL, 60610.

Karen Pierce, M.D., Director, Children's Outpatient Services
Rush-Presbyterian St. Luke's Hospital, Chicago, Illinois

My name is Amanda Martha. I live in a house with my mama, my daddy, and a cat named Alfred, Lord of the Alley. I wanted a cat for a long time before I got Alfred, or Alfred got me. It's hard to say which way it happened.

We have sad days, glad days, mostly in-between days at my house. Sad days are when my mama doesn't hear me. Her ears can hear me. It is inside her that she doesn't hear me. She goes away from me even though she's still there. She says she feels like darkness comes over her. She wears her blue bathrobe all day. Sometimes she's angry with me for no reason. She cries, and I don't know why.

I get cold cereal to eat. I hate cold cereal. It's sad food.

Mama's not always sad. When she feels better, we have fun.

We make animal pancakes. She's good at rabbits. I'm great at turtles. One morning I asked her, "Why do you get sad and cry? Do I make you sad?"

She told me, "Amanda Martha, it's not your fault when I sleep all day and feel sad and cry. It's important for you to remember: I have something called depression."

And I asked, "What's depression?"

"It's a sickness you can't see. On the outside of me I don't look sick, but the depression affects my body, my mood, and my thoughts. Sometimes I feel like I'm trying to swim in thick syrup."

"Icky," I said.

"It *is* icky. And I can't just make it go away, like shooing a fly out of the house."

"I can help you," I told Mama.

She shook her head. "It's not your job or Daddy's to help me not feel sad. It is the job of doctors and other people who are trained to help me. There is medicine I take, too."

Mama smiled. "You don't have to feel sad and gloomy because I do. It's all right for you to be happy."

"When you get sad, I feel like I'm all alone," I say. "Someday will you leave me by myself and not come back?"

She answered, "No, I will always come back. Even when I am sad, you are my Amanda Martha, my cuddliest cuddle muffin in all the world."

In the afternoon, I went to
Alice's house to play. Alice had
a new kitten. We patted its fur.
The kitten purred as if it had a
soft motor inside it.

When Daddy came home, I told him about Alice's kitten. I asked if I could have one.

"I think a pet's more work than your mama feels she can handle right now," said Daddy. "So the answer is no."

Daddy says it's all right when I say I want another mama. He understands if I feel that way. Sometimes he feels angry when he comes home and our house is a mess. "Mama loves us," Daddy tells me. "She feels bad, and she feels bad again for feeling bad. She doesn't want to be depressed any more than somebody wants warts."

Daddy and I made up a game we play about what color Mama's mood is on different days. We pretend there is a giant thermometer with colors on it instead of numbers. I draw it with my crayons. The colors go from black to bright yellow. I say she was blue today, or maybe she got down to deep purple or up to pink.

He says, "You know how it is, Amanda Martha."

I say, "I know. It's glad days, sad days, mostly in-between days."

Daddy says, "Maybe she'll be in the pink tomorrow."

The next day was an almost-pink day. Mama and I
sat on the back steps. She read poems from her book by
Alfred, Lord Tennyson. She says she only reads the
short poems. I drew pictures of alligators because that's
what I draw best. I asked again if I could have a kitten.
Mama said no. Just no.

I asked, "May I have a goldfish? Just a little
goldfish?"

Mama closed her book and said, "I think a goldfish
is a good idea."

"I'd rather have a kitten that can purr," I told her.

Mama sighed. "My cuddle muffin, there are days
when I have so little energy I feel as if I can barely
move, much less take care of a messy kitten."

"Alice's mother let her have a kitten. I can help take
care of a kitten on sad days, and you help me when
you have in-between and glad days."

Mama leaned forward and put her elbows on her
knees. "You really want a kitten, don't you? Well, for
now I think a goldfish is better."

So Mama and I went to the pet store. I named my goldfish Lightning. He could swim fast, but he was still a scaly fish and not a kitten.

Walking home, we saw Mrs. Henderson digging around her roses. Mrs. Henderson's cats were rolling in the catmint she plants under her roses. Sometimes I go to Mrs. Henderson's house when Mama has a sad day. I help her pull weeds in her garden.

She smiled like she always does. "Good morning, Amanda Martha. I haven't seen much of you lately."

Mama smiled, too. She said, "Your roses are looking beautiful."

Mrs. Henderson cut some yellow roses for Mama.

We were almost at our back door when we heard yowling
from the alley like tigers roaring in the deep jungle. Then the
wild howling stopped. A big orange cat came strutting along
the top of the fence. His tail waved like a banner. Mama said,
"Look at that cat. He's like the Lord of the Alley looking over
his lands."

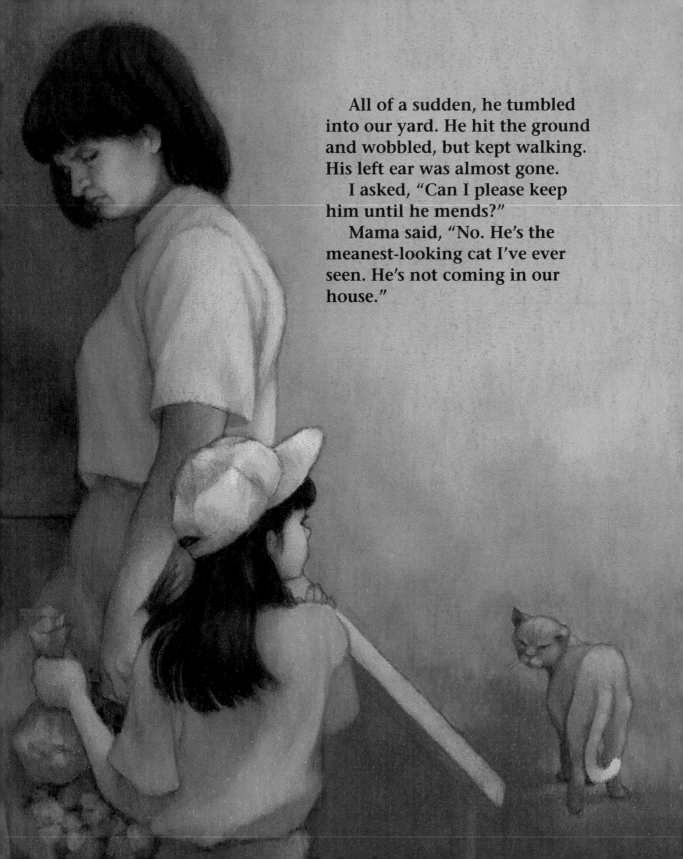

All of a sudden, he tumbled into our yard. He hit the ground and wobbled, but kept walking. His left ear was almost gone.

I asked, "Can I please keep him until he mends?"

Mama said, "No. He's the meanest-looking cat I've ever seen. He's not coming in our house."

The next day was a sad day. Mama
poured me cold cereal for breakfast,
and I went to sit on the back steps to
eat it. An orange tail with a white tip
peeked out from under Mrs.
Henderson's thornless rosebush. I
walked over to look through the
tangled canes. There was that cat. He
was hungry. I put my bowl of sad-day
cold cereal on the ground. He lapped
it up. I decided Alfred was a good
name to call him.

Mama said I could put cereal for Alfred in the alley, but he couldn't come in the house—ever. I fed Alfred for a lot of days before he could walk again. One day when we sat on the steps, Alfred pranced across the yard looking wonderful. Mama said, "That cat looks like he really is the Lord of the Alley today."

I said, "He's not awful looking now. Can I keep him?"

Mama sighed and didn't answer me.

Alfred was carrying something grey in his mouth. I walked toward him.

When I saw what it was, I screamed. Alfred dropped the dead mouse at my feet. And then he sat there looking proud of himself.

Mama stood and stared at Alfred. Then she came up beside me and said softly, "My most beloved cuddle muffin in all the world, if you want that cat you can keep him. We can take care of him together." I saw tears coming into her eyes. These weren't her sad tears. These were happy tears from down in her heart where she loves me most of all.

After supper, we made a bed for Alfred in the corner of my room. He got on it and purred—louder than any little kitten could purr.

When I was in bed, I asked Mama, "Why did you change your mind? How come Alfred gets to live with us after he brought me a yucky dead mouse?"

She said, "You took care of Alfred. The very best present Alfred can give you is the mouse he caught. And the very best present I can give you is a brave cat like Alfred."

It's like I said. At my house we have sad days, glad days, mostly in-between days—and some days I will never forget.